# Bess and Bella

Other books by Irene Haas


*A Summertime Song*

*The Maggie B.*

*Little Moon Theater*

(Margaret K. McElderry Books)

# Bess and Bella

by Irene Haas

Margaret K. McElderry Books

NEW YORK   LONDON   TORONTO   SYDNEY

Margaret K. McElderry Books
An imprint of Simon & Schuster Children's Publishing Division
1230 Avenue of the Americas, New York, New York 10020
Book design by Ann Bobco
The text for this book is set in Filosofia.
The illustrations for this book are rendered in watercolor with some pastel.
Manufactured in the United States of America
10 9 8 7 6 5 4 3 2 1
Library of Congress Cataloging-in-Publication Data
Haas, Irene.
Bess and Bella / by Irene Haas.—1st ed.
p. cm.
Summary: Bess is feeling terribly lonely when out of the sky tumbles a bird named Bella,
her tiny suitcases packed with all manner of wonderful things.
ISBN 1-4169-0013-6 (ISBN-13: 978-1-4169-0013-9) (hardcover)
[1. Loneliness—Fiction. 2. Friendship—Fiction. 3. Birds—Fiction.] I. Title.
PZ7.H1128Be 2006
[E]—dc22
2004012732

*For Miranda and Mitchell*

It was a cold winter afternoon.
Bess was outside, talking to her doll.
"Rose," she said, "doesn't it seem there's no one in the world
but you and me?"

Bess sighed and wished for a friend to play with.

*A cookie might cheer me up,* Bess thought.
She looked in her pockets,
but all she could find were crumbs.
So she made a tea party
with cookie crumbs and melted snow tea.

Sipping from a little cracked cup,
Bess asked Rose, "Do you think we will have more snow?"
Rose fell off her chair.
Her eyes stared up at the sky,
so Bess looked up too.

Something was up there!
Bess watched it tumbling down through the clouds.
She watched as it landed FALUMP on the ground
into some powdery snow.

It was a little bird
fluffing itself, trying to stand up.
Tiny suitcases were scattered everywhere.
"Hello!" peeped the bird.
"My name is Bella!"

Bess asked Bella to tea.
When Bella saw the crumbs
and the little cracked cup
of melted snow,
she said, "Excuse me, please,"
and she got up from the table.

She opened a tiny suitcase.
Out came wonderful things:
babushkas for tablecloths, a teapot of tea,
a beautiful bowl of just-baked buttery biscuits. . . .

Then Bella told her story.
"It was time to fly south for the winter," she said.
"So I packed
and I packed
and I packed all my things,
and then it was too late to fly.
But I flew anyhow—
until frost on my wings
made me fall FALUMP from the sky."

"Oh, Bella, your story is thrilling!" said Bess.
She spread cherry jam on a biscuit and wondered,
*What story can I tell Bella?*
But before she could say a word,
a fire truck clanged down the street,
carrying a man with his hat on fire.

Five little firefighters hopped off the truck,
taking charge of their fire-fighting duty.
They watered the flames,
which turned into flowers,
and they gave the flowers to Bess.
Bess asked them all to tea.

When they finished their tea,
the firefighters didn't go home.
So Bella opened a suitcase.
Out came a whistle, a watering can, a banjo,
a bugle, a frying pan—
and suddenly there was music!

Bess couldn't wait to sing.
She began, "Old MacDonald had a farm . . . ,"
but somebody cried,
"STOP THE MUSIC!"

A mouse and her children were huddled there,
whiskers all wet with tears.
"I've lost a child!"
the mother mouse wept.
"I don't know what to do!"
The firefighters went to the rescue.
They found the mouse baby safe and sound,
sleeping in Rose's bed.

Bess asked the mouse family to tea.
But there was nothing left to eat.
So Bella opened a suitcase.
Out came six bowls, six little spoons,
and a jar of golden jam.
All the mouse children
whipped up in a trice
a marvelous marmalade mousse for mice.
The party went merrily on.

Then it began to snow.
Everyone was quiet, watching the fat flakes fall.
Everyone heard a voice call, "Bess!
It's suppertime, Bess, come home!"

The firefighters clanged away.
The mice scurried down their hole.
Bess put Bella in a soft woolly mitten
and carried her home to her room.

Bella stayed all winter,
helping Bess with schoolwork,
watching a little TV,
singing songs—
until one day it was spring,
when birds return to their nests.

And when Bess stood at her window
to watch Bella fly away,
she heard someone down on the sidewalk call up,
"Hi! Do you want to play?"